THE Twelve Days of Christmas

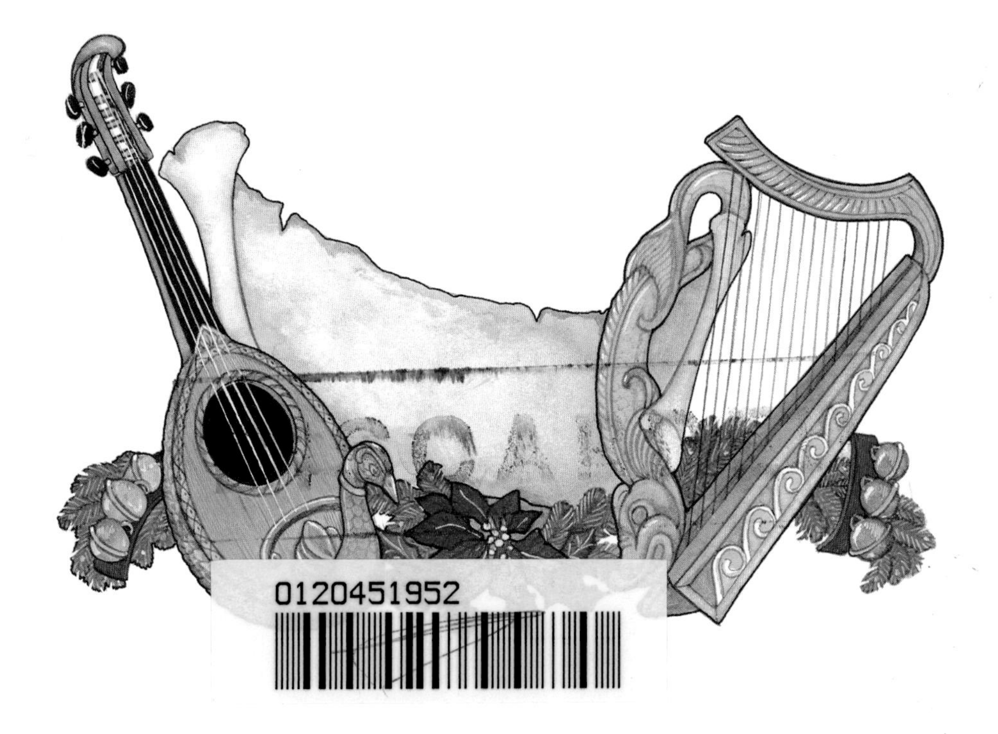

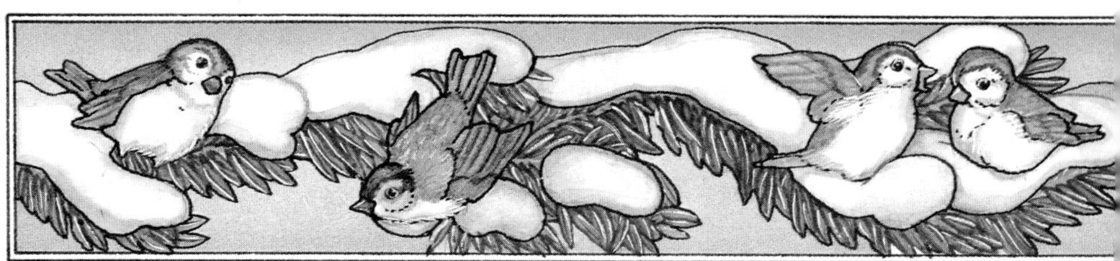

THE Twelve

For Lia

Illustrated by JAN BRETT

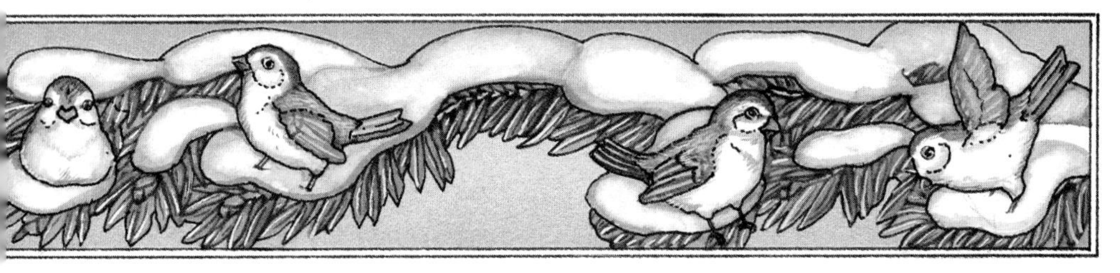

Days of
Christmas

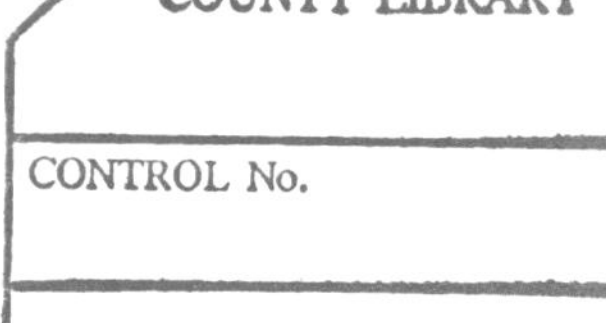

MACDONALD YOUNG BOOKS

THE TWELVE DAYS

English traditional carol
VERSES 1-4
1. On the first* day of Christ-mas my
2. On the se-cond* day of Christ-mas my
true love gave to me a
true love gave to me
4
3
2
1
four col-ly birds, three French_hens, two tur-tle-doves,
four three _ two
and a par-tridge_in a pear tree.
VERSES 5-12
5. On the fifth* day of Christ-mas my true love gave to me
6. On the sixth* day of Christ-mas my true love gave to me
12
twelve lords a-leap-ing,
twelve

Sing appropriate number of day, and then cut from † to appropriate boxed number.

OF CHRISTMAS

11
10
e-lev'n la-dies danc-ing, ten pi-pers pi-ping,
e-lev'n ten
9
8
nine drum-mers drum-ming, eight maids a-milk-ing,
nine eight
7
6
5
sev'n swans a-swim-ming, six geese a-lay-ing,
sev'n six five gold rings, four___col - ly birds,
three French hens, two___ tur - tle-doves, and a par - tridge___ in a pear tree.

Merry

On the first day of Christmas

Christmas

My true love gave to me
A partridge in a pear tree.

Buon

On the second day of Christmas
My true love gave to me

Natale

Two turtledoves,
And a partridge in a pear tree.

Joyeux

On the third day of Christmas
My true love gave to me
Three French hens,

Noël

Two turtledoves,
And a partridge in a pear tree.

GOD

On the fourth day of Christmas
My true love gave to me
Four colly birds,

JUL!

Three French hens,
Two turtledoves,
And a partridge in a pear tree.

ZALIGE

On the fifth day of Christmas
My true love gave to me
Five gold rings,
Four colly birds,

KERSTDAGEN

Three French hens,
Two turtledoves,
And a partridge in a pear tree.

Wesołego

On the sixth day of Christmas
My true love gave to me
Six geese a-laying,
Five gold rings,

Four colly birds,
Three French hens,
Two turtledoves,
And a partridge in a pear tree.

СЧАСТЛИВОГО

On the seventh day of Christmas
My true love gave to me
Seven swans a-swimming,
Six geese a-laying,
Five gold rings,

Four colly birds,
Three French hens,
Two turtledoves,
And a partridge in a pear tree.

FRÖHLICHE

On the eighth day of Christmas
My true love gave to me
Eight maids a-milking,
Seven swans a-swimming,
Six geese a-laying,

Five gold rings,
Four colly birds,
Three French hens,
Two turtledoves,
And a partridge in a pear tree.

Boldog
Karácsonyi

On the ninth day of Christmas
My true love gave to me
Nine drummers drumming,
Eight maids a-milking,
Seven swans a-swimming,
Six geese a-laying,

Five gold rings,
Four colly birds,
Three French hens,
Two turtledoves,
And a partridge in a pear tree.

Nollaig

On the tenth day of Christmas
My true love gave to me
Ten pipers piping,
Nine drummers drumming,
Eight maids a-milking,
Seven swans a-swimming,

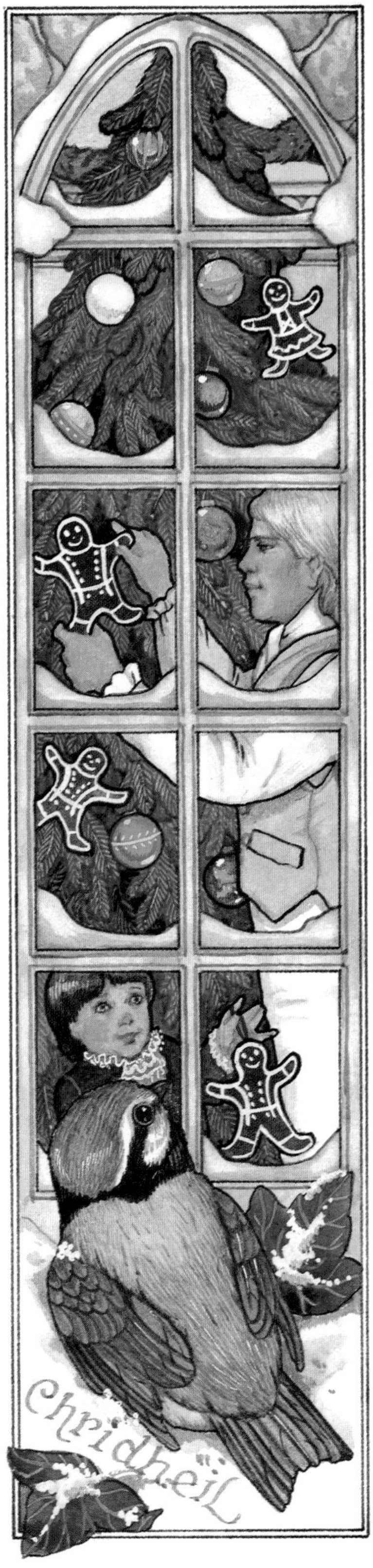

Six geese a-laying,
Five gold rings,
Four colly birds,
Three French hens,
Two turtledoves,
And a partridge in a pear tree.

On the eleventh day of Christmas
My true love gave to me
Eleven ladies dancing,
Ten pipers piping,
Nine drummers drumming,
Eight maids a-milking,
Seven swans a-swimming,

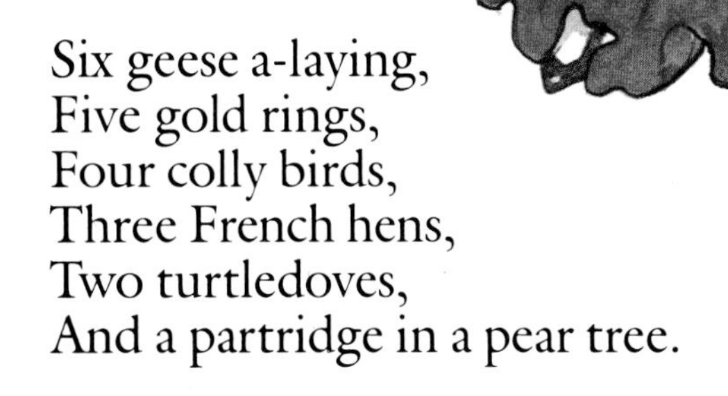

Six geese a-laying,
Five gold rings,
Four colly birds,
Three French hens,
Two turtledoves,
And a partridge in a pear tree.

Happy

On the twelfth day of Christmas
My true love gave to me
Twelve lords a-leaping,
Eleven ladies dancing,
Ten pipers piping,
Nine drummers drumming,
Eight maids a-milking,

New Year!

Seven swans a-swimming,
Six geese a-laying,
Five gold rings,
Four colly birds,
Three French hens,
Two turtledoves,
And a partridge in a pear tree.

Editor's Note

The Twelve Days of Christmas—the days linking Christmas on December 25 and the Epiphany on January 6 (when the three Magi offered the first Christmas presents—gold, frankincense, and myrrh) were declared a festal tide (religious holiday) by the Council of Tours in 567. Since then it has been a time when noble and peasant alike put work aside and enjoyed an extended holiday of feasting, celebration, and sharing with others. It was considered bad luck to enter someone's house empty-handed.

The ancient counting song named for this religious holiday is actually quite pagan in tone and is the only carol we know that celebrates, in the form of a list, the Christmas tradition of gift-giving. It is said to date back to a thirteenth century manuscript in the Library of Trinity College, Cambridge, England. The carol appeared in print for the first time in a children's book entitled, *Mirth Without Mischief,* published in London about 1780.

"The Twelve Days of Christmas" became very popular as a game song—usually played at a large gathering of children and adults on the Twelfth Day night, just before the eating of mince pie. With the company seated all around the room, the leader of the game began by singing the first day lines, which were then repeated by each of the company in turn. Then the first day lines were repeated with the addition of the second day lines by the leader, and this was repeated by all in turn. This continued until all the lines of the twelve days were repeated by everyone. If anyone missed a line, they would have to forfeit something of theirs to the group.

First published in Great Britain in 1987 by Beehive Books, an imprint of
Macdonald & Co. (Publishers) Limited
First published in paperback in 1989 by
Macdonald Young Books
61 Western Road
Hove
East Sussex
BN3 1JD

This edition published in 1999 by Macdonald Young Books

Original American edition published by Dodd, Mead & Company, Inc.,
New York, N.Y., USA

Printed and bound in Hong Kong by Toppan

British Library cataloguing in Publication Data available

ISBN: 0 7500 2868 8